ALABASTER SHADOWS

AN ONI PRESS PUBLICATION

ALABAST

ER SHADOWS

written by MATT GARDNER

illustrated by RASHAD DOUCET

lettered by RYAN FERRIER

designed by HILARY THOMPSON

edited by JILL BEATON & ROBIN HERRERA

color flatting assistance by JONATHAN MULLINS

PUBLISHED BY ONI PRESS, INC.

publisher JOE NOZEMACK
editor in chief JAMES LUCAS JONES
director of sales CHEYENNE ALLOTT
director of publicity FRED RECKLING
production manager TROY LOOK
graphic designer HILARY THOMPSON
production assistant JARED JONES
senior editor CHARLIE CHU
editor ROBIN HERRERA
associate editor ARI YARWOOD
inventory coordinator BRAD ROOKS
office assistant JUNG LEE

onipress.com
facebook.com/onipress
twitter.com/onipress
onipress.tumblr.com
instagram.com/onipress

First Edition: December 2015

ISBN 978-1-62010-264-0
eISBN 978-1-62010-265-7

Alabaster Shadows, December, 2015. Published by Oni Press, Inc. 1305 SE Martin Luther King Jr. Blvd., Suite A, Portland, OR 97214.

Printed in China.

Library of Congress Control Number: 2015909439

1 2 3 4 5 6 7 8 9 10

Here we are, kids.
WELCOME TO ALABASTER SHADOWS

Welcome to our new home.

All of the houses look the same.

How do we know which one is ours?

They only look the same because you're not used to it yet, Carter.

You love exploring, think of it as a whole new set of adventures just waiting to be found.
Just give it some time, kids.

Before long, you'll know this place like the back of your hands.

If you say so.

As soon as I can find the rest of the paperwork we can get everything finalized so you can move into your new home.

We're very much looking forward to joining such a pleasant-looking community.
Good to hear.

I want to make sure your transition goes as smoothly as... where did I put those papers?

I'm sure we and the kids will feel right at home in no time.

Ah, the children!

And these must be them.
Yes, of course. This is Carter and Polly. Say hello to the nice man, kids.

Um, hello, sir.
HI!

Why hello, children! I'd like to make sure you both know that children are always welcome here in—

Mr. Randolph, I have the new resident paperwork.

Ah, thank you. What would I do without you?

This is Miss Crowe, she's the head of the Community Council.
Yes, the Community Council governs community events and spending.

We also ensure that all of our residents follow proper ordinances regarding acceptable home use and maintenance...
...and that they conduct themselves in a proper neighborly fashion befitting such a community.
But please...

...call me Priscilla.

You must be the Normandys.

And these must be the children.

I trust they won't prove to be too much of a nuisance.

Miss Crowe will assist you with the rest of the paperwork and give you your keys.

Please, step into my office. The children can wait here.

Polly, be a dear and wait here with your brother until we're done.

So... are you kids excited to see your new home?

Does it look like all the other houses?

Heh, it probably does.
Awwww.

Are there any other kids here?
Of course there are.

We even have our own school, I'm sure you'll make plenty of friends there.

Miss Crowe doesn't like kids, does she?

Maybe not.

She just doesn't realize quite how important children like you are to this place.
My mommy says that when I grow up I could be as important as the president, or a unicorn!

That may be true, but you don't need to wait to grow up to be important.

Listen, if either of you see anything strange or out of the ordinary, anything at all, remember that you can come here and talk to me.

Like what? A house that doesn't look just like all the others?
No, he means like purple grass, dummy.

You should know it if you see it.

Now, if you'll excuse me, I must get back to my work. Your parents should be finished very soon.

He was weird.
Polly, he's right there!

But he is!
He said to tell him if you saw something strange.

Maybe you should go tell him how weird he is?
Eek! No!

If you don't mind, there are adults in here trying to conduct business!

Carter, hurry up and get ready for school!

You don't want to be late to your first day.

I'm just trying to find my bag! I'll be up in a sec!
TOYS
UP
U-BOX

S.P.K.O.

TOYS
U-BOX

What was that?

Nothing.

U-BOX
U-BOX

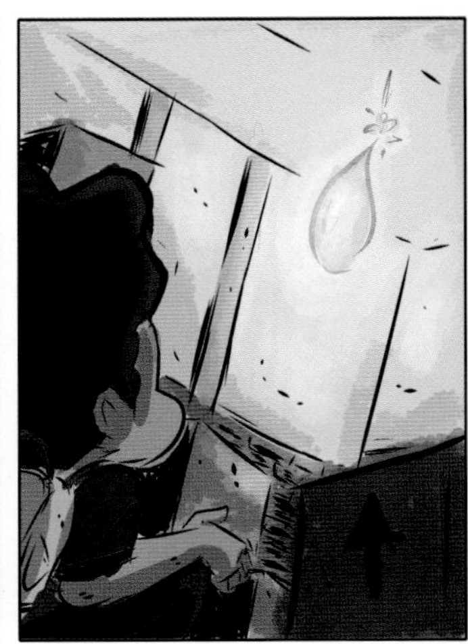

Is that water?
U-BOX

Carter! You're going to be late!
SPKO

Mom, I think there's some sort of leak in the basement.

Don't worry, honey. We can have a plumber stop by if we need to.

But there's not any pipes or anything.
I'm waiting!

I'm sure it's nothing your father and I can't handle.

Now both of you hurry off to school.
Bye, mom!

LEARN
...so the smaller number is called an exponent.
MATH
DON'T BE TARDY
READ!

It represents the number of times you multiply a number by itself...

She's a member of the Council!

What?
Ms. Frump, the teacher. She's a part of the Community Council.

Everyone in the Council hates children. It's like what they do.

Miss Wayland. Do you have something you wish to share with the class?
No, Ms. Frump, ma'am.

Good. We don't want to fill anyone else's heads with your ridiculous nonsense.

As I was saying, when you multiply a number by itself...

See what I mean?

If she hates children, why does she teach at the school?
Beats me, probably to keep an eye on us. "Know your enemy" and all that.

Mr. Normandy!!

Would you like to spend the rest of your first day of class in detention?
Uh, no, ma'am.
I'd recommend keeping that in mind next time you want to speak during lessons.

That's lunch, children. Everybody be back in your seats by next bell or there will be an extra assignment for everyone tonight!

"Bigfoot Found in Consignment Store."
I can't believe you still read that thing.
And that's because you're boring.

Hi, I'm Harley. This is my boring brother, Warren.
I'm Carter. My family just moved here.
How do you like it so far?
It's alright, I guess.
MATH

Actually... there is one thing.

Have either of you noticed anything... strange around here?
Not really, no. Everything's always pretty ordinary.
Unless you count Dudley.

Harley!
What? I think he counts as strange.
Who's Dudley?
MATH

He's right over there.
Nobody talks to him, he just sits there and draws on his desk all day.

That's probably because nobody talks to him.
Well, I suppose that's—

I'm going to go say hi.

Hi.
Hi.

I'm Carter.
I'm Dudley.

What're you drawing?
One of the monsters from under my bed.

Mom! Dad! We're home!
How was your first day?

School was awesome! The teacher taught about math and I told her I already know math and she was sooooooo impressed!

That's great, Polly!

Oh Carter, I called the lady from the Community Council and she sent a gentleman down to fix that leak in the basement.

So nice to get such a quick response.
Did you see it?

Your father and I have been so busy unpacking, we haven't even made it downstairs yet. But the man from the Council said it should be as good as new.
SUPER

U-BOX

It's gone?
U-BOX
U-BOX
U-BOX
U-BOX

Wait...

The mortar isn't dry?
This wall is new!

It's still there!

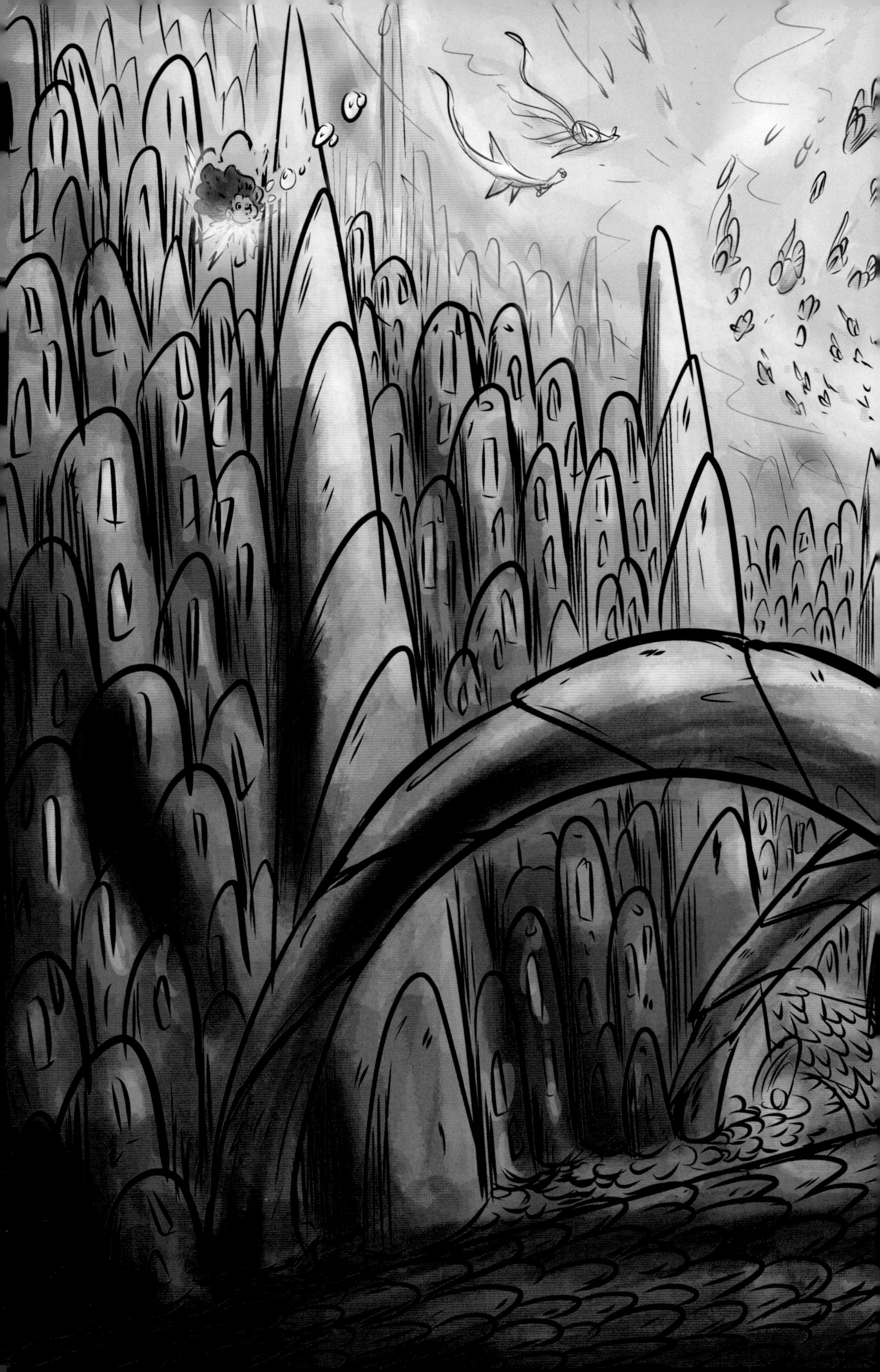

Woah.

EAT!
TRASH
Ha ha ha ha ha ha ha ha ha!

Okay, say it again.
I'm serious! There's some sort of portal to an underwater city in my basement!

Carter, think about it logically. If there were some sort of two-way opening to someplace underwater there'd be water pouring out all over the place.

There is!
Oh.

The monsters under my bed live in an underwater city.

They talk about it all the time.

They talk to you?
Not to me, no.
I don't think they know I can hear them.

I don't know why you find this so hard to believe, Harley. Is this any more unbelievable than the stuff in that magazine of yours?

There is an important difference between you and the Weekly Journal of Truth: photographic evidence!
You can't be serious. Any of those photos can be fakes.

Pics or it didn't happen.
Argh!

Actually... I've got a picture that I can't explain. It's not an underwater city or anything, but...
What?!

I didn't want to bring it up because I know there's a perfectly logical explanation for it...

...I just haven't yet figured out what it is.

I've never seen buildings that... angular.
Where is this?
I'm not sure.
Then where did you take it, genius?

That's the weird part...
DO YOUR BEST
"I was in band class, waiting for my part in the song.
"I guess I dozed off or something.
"The next thing I know I'm dreaming about this crazy city with all these weird buildings.
"I look around a bit and take a picture.
"Then I wake up back in class."

I didn't even notice until later that the picture was still on my phone.
Woah.
Perhaps it's one of the default pictures?

We have the same model phone and I don't have that picture.
Still, I'm sure there's a reasonable explanation.

No way. This is too awesome for a reasonable explanation.
Maybe this is what Mr. Randolph was talking about.
Who?
That guy who works in the welcoming center, he said to tell him if I saw anything weird.
I thought he was just a little loopy but now I'm not so sure.

What are you talking about?
There's something strange going on around here, and now we've got proof.
It's a picture, it's not proof of anything!
It's definitely something.

Meet me after school, we need to show this to him. He might be able to tell us something about it.

Hello, welcome to the Alabaster–

Oh, it's you. The Normandy child. Why are you here?

We want to talk to Mr. Randolph.
Mr. Randolph is a very busy man.
It's important. We have something to show him.

Listen, I am far too busy to waste my time with infants. I'm sure Mr. Randolph would not appreciate–

That's alright, Miss Crowe. Send them in.

Mr. Randolph will see you in his office.

Hello Carter, I see you've brought friends. I trust you've all been keeping your eyes open.

There's a lot out there to see, though much of it may not want to be seen.
You told me to tell you if I saw anything unusual and I think we've—
What's that supposed to mean?

Children and adults alike must be careful when they speak.

You never know who may be listening.

Look at this, is this the sort of thing you were talking about?

Who took this?

Well I... I mean, we still don't know exactly what... I'm sure there's a perfectly reasonable...

Dreams can be a funny thing. Sometimes it's hard to tell when you're still in your own or not.

Wait, what?
Do you know something about that picture?
Mr. Randolph.

You are due for your appointment at the school.

I'm sorry, children. But I cannot stay. Come back any time.

And remember, when things seem impossible to understand, sometimes all you need is the right tool.

We do not offer a day care here. You're going to have to find somewhere else to play.

That was a complete waste of time!
What a weirdo. And he gave me this stupid ring. What's this supposed to be?
It looks like he recognized that picture.

Don't you see, guys? He definitely knows something! He just couldn't say anything because Miss Crowe was listening!

Well then he should have written it down.
I'm sure she can read.

You're all making a big deal out of nothing. He's clearly just some crazy old man who spends too much time cooped up in that tiny office. We should just forget about it and go home.

Even if he is crazy, there's still something going on! What about that thing in my basement?

Maybe you're just crazy too, hah!
I'll show it to you!

I'm not getting dragged all over the place to appease some fantasy!
It's not like we've got anything else to do.

You don't seriously believe this, do you?
What do you say, Dudley?

I kinda want to see it.

Three to one, Warr.
Argh!

Come on, my place is this way.

It's behind here.

There.

See? Just like I told you.

It's probably just a leaky pipe.

It's coming from thin air! It's not a pipe!
You promised a city, I just see some dripping water.

Fine, just stand over here.

And hold your breath.

Ready?
Whatever, it's just–

That's awesome! We've got to go in there and check it out.
No way I'm going through that, what if we can't get back out? We'd be trapped.

If the water can come out, I imagine we could, too.
That settles it! We're going!

If it really is underwater, how do you expect to breathe?
I don't know. Do I have to think of everything?
I've got it!
U-BOX

I'm sure we've got some garden hoses packed up–

Here!

But there's only two.
Great, we can stay here where it's dry.
U-BOX

Fine, but be ready to pull us out if anything happens.

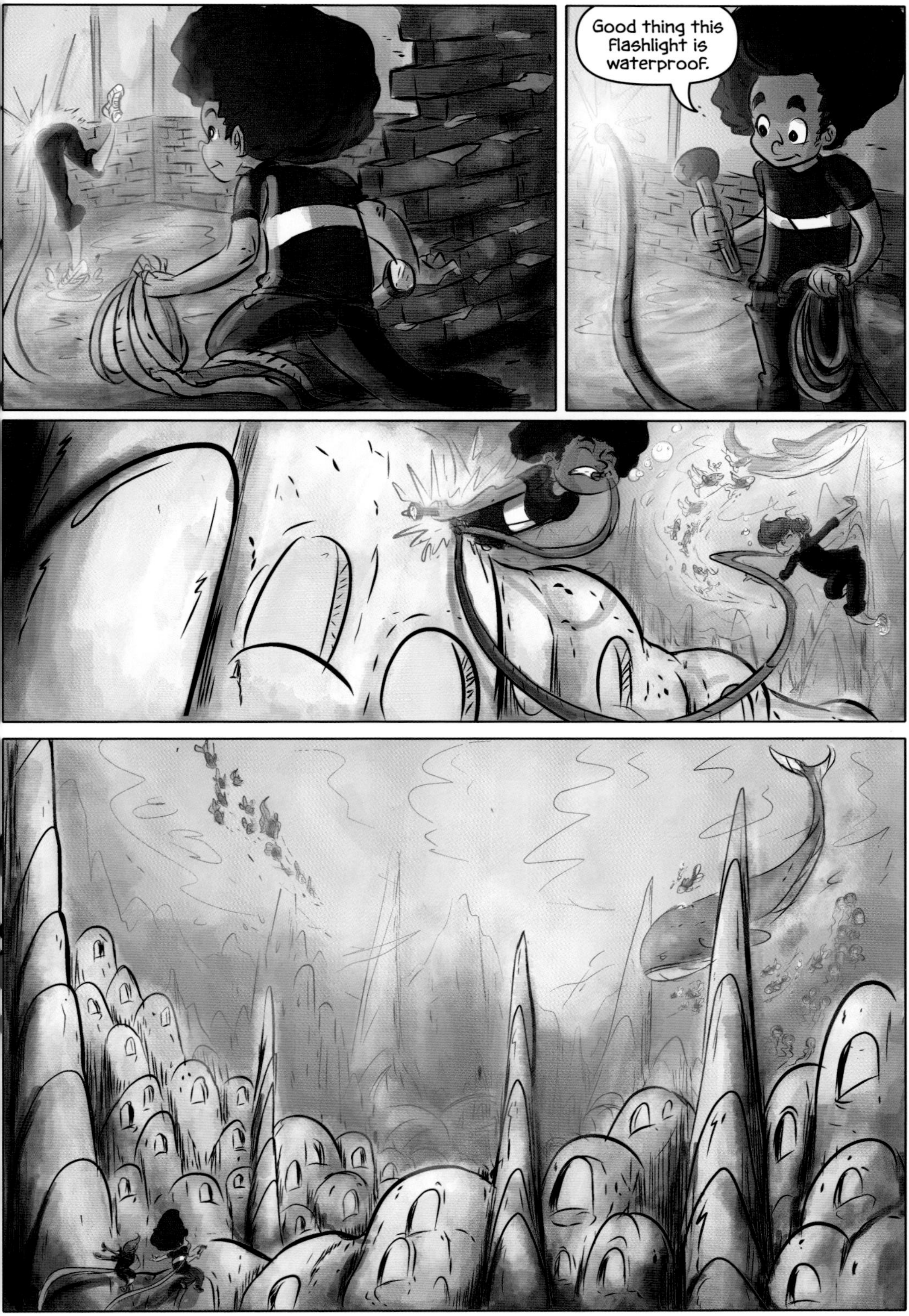

Good thing this flashlight is waterproof.

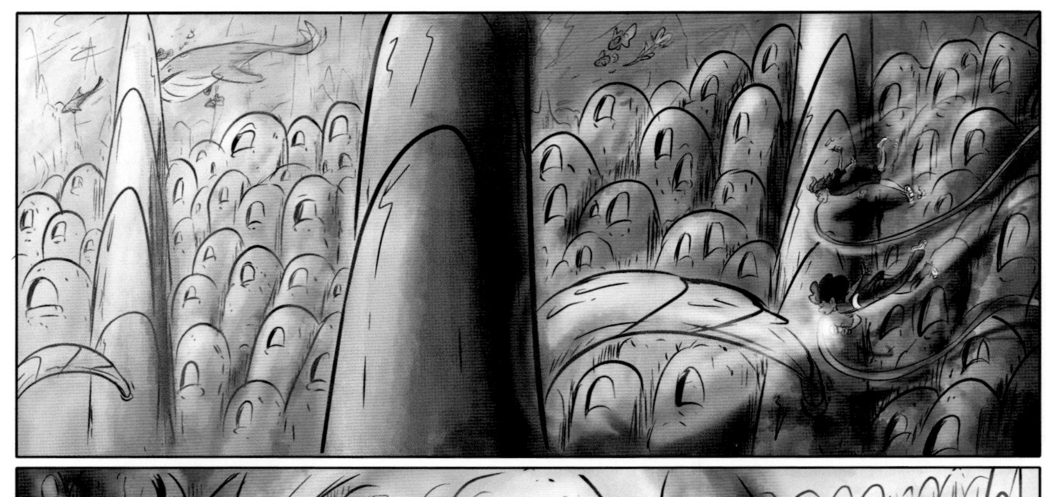

PLOP!

It's dry?
This is so cool!

Guys, can you hear me?

There's a building here full of air, we're taking a look around.

But that's impossible!
Warren, you idiot. Don't you ever listen?

Nothing's impossible! Especially when it's awesome!

You didn't believe me about there being an underwater city in my basement.
You should've taken a picture.

I don't have an underwater camera.
And how is that my fault?

Hey, look at that!

A book?
Bleh. Boring.

I can't
read any of what
this says, it's just
gibberish.

Well let's take it.
Warren reads a lot of
books, maybe he can
make something
of it.
We can't just
take it, what if it
belongs to somebody?

Do you
see anyone
else here?
Alright,
fine. Guys, we
found some weird
book down
here...

We're coming back up.
Carter, behind you! What is that!

We're not falling for it, sis.
It's got my legs! Quick, pull us back!
We've got to get them out!

Fine, but don't blame me when Harley calls you a sucker.
Shut up and get us out of here!

See, Dudley. I told you there was nothing.

And she swings!

Ew, it's all squishy!
Whatever it is I don't like it!
A little help here?!
On it!

Carter, where's your kitchen?
What?
Why are you thinking of food?!
Bludgeons are obviously ineffective and one of us needs to think rationally.
Rationally?! Oh great, hitting it doesn't work so let's try making a canape!
Carter?
Uh, up the stairs and to the left.
Thank you.

Ack!

C'mon, you, pay attention to me!
Ack! Get off of me!
I can't hold on.

When the barbarians in Phys Ed are at a loss...
SALT
BRAND

...It's time for Home Ec and a bit of science.

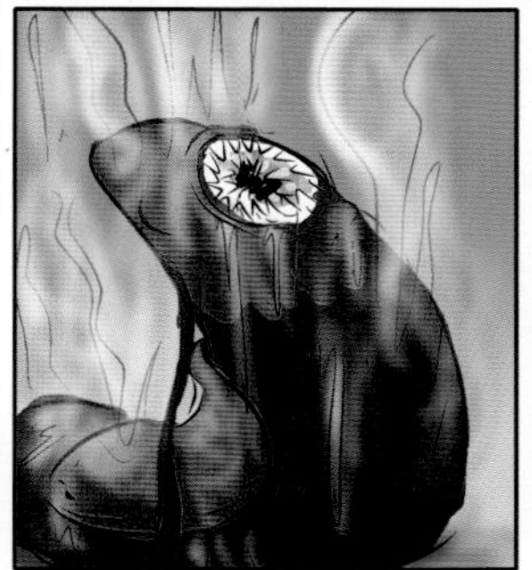

That was awesome, Warren.
What was that?
Salt. This creature is obviously some sort of gastropod mollusk.

What?
A slug, though I'm not certain which species.
Species?!

Don't be stupid. It's some kind of monster. Monsters don't have species!
Now who's being stupid? Just because it's unusual doesn't mean that there isn't a perfectly reasonable explanation for it.

What kind of reasonable explanation could there possibly be?!
U-BOX
I'm with Harley on this one.

There's a giant underwater city in my basement. And it's apparently filled with giant slug monsters. How do you begin to explain that?
It's just like you to jump to ridiculous conclusions.

Carter!

Mom and I just got back from the store and–
U-BOX

What are you doing down here?
Uh...

We're uh... just looking for...

This lava lamp! Found it!

U-BOX
Hey, that's mine! Give it back!

Eeeeew! What smells like fish?!

Mom says dinner is in ten minutes. You better not stink up the food!

Phew.
What do we do with this thing?

We can't just leave it here.

This thing is heavier than it looks.

What do we do if something else comes through?!

I've got this.

There.

That's... uh...
It stopped the leak.

Do you believe me now?
It's hard to argue at this point.
But what do we do now?

Mr. Randolph. It's me, Carter Normandy!

I don't think he's here.
They're still supposed to be open.

He's obviously not answering. Warren, give me your bus pass.
I don't know that this is a good idea.

Are we sure this is the sort of thing he meant when he said "anything strange"?

Maybe he was just talking about someone trying to break into a car or building.

Sorta like we're doing now.
Got it!

Hello?

I still don't think he's here.

Looks like they closed early.
His office light is on!

Looks like he's in here.

Mr. Randolph?

writhing ichor-drenched appendages of indescribable texture
innumerable throngs of nameless beasts with nearly human lineage

I remember him being a bit more... lively.
Something's wrong.
translucent ever-moving tendrils

He's completely unresponsive. Dudley's right, he's not here.
What could have happened to him?
utmost unknowable blackness

I definitely think this counts as "something strange."
We should really get out of here before—
He was fine before.
I don't like this at all.

You children shouldn't be carelessly milling about without supervision.

I would hate to have to tell your parents if something awful were to occur.

Now tell me what you are doing here.

We wanted to talk with Mr. Randolph.

As you can see, Mr. Randolph has been working very hard.

He's going to be taking a sabbatical, a sort of "mental break" if you will.

Let us leave him be so that we don't disturb his much-needed rest.

Now...

What was it you wished to speak with Mr. Randolph about?

I can assure you that the Community Council is prepared to address anything that may concern you.

The first thing that concerns me is—

We just wanted to say "hi." Nothing, really.
We'll leave you to your work, I'm sure you're very busy.

Yes, indeed.

Okay, now I'm freaked out. What the heck did Miss Crowe do to Mr. Randolph?
We don't know that it was her.
She sure didn't seem bothered by it.

He was trying to warn us about her! She's got something to do with what's going on, why else would she want to get him out of the way?

But she's the head of the Community Council. Granted they're a bunch of kid-hating geezers but what could they have to do with slug monsters in your basement?

I don't know. But she did have someone try to hide the leak.

It just doesn't make any sense!
Finally, someone agrees with me!
Shut up, Warren, you're not helping.
Uh, guys?

From the looks of it, Mr. Randolph won't be able to help us anymore.
About the only thing we've got to go on is this book we found.

Have you figured out how to open it?
No, it's still stuck tight.

Then let's get this book to the library.
Since when do you go to the library?

I've got an idea.

This is your idea?

SWANG!

It worked.

Let's see what it says.
Can you read it?
It's not in English.
Well, of course they don't speak English underwater.

Look at that! It's one of those things Dudley keeps drawing!
What?!

Dudley! Let me see your sketchbook.

What did you say this was, Dudley?
It's, uh..

It's one of the monsters under my bed.

READ
No way!

What else is in here?

Gasp

Now that's what I call a monster!

There's some sort of writing here, but I have no idea what it says.
We don't know the language, it's impossible for us to understand it.

That's it! The ring Mr. Randolph gave you!
What about it?

He said when things seem impossible to understand, you just need the right tool. Maybe that's why he gave you the ring!

Don't be ridiculous. It's just a plain old ring, see?
What could it possibly do to help us understand this stuff?

Then why are you so nervous?
I'm not!

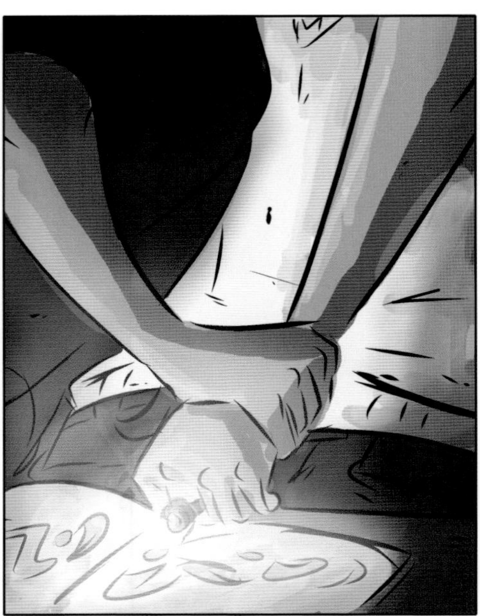

Woah!

Grown men who looked into its eyes were instantly driven mad.

They had to abandon the great city of Wa'Taar and live in the shadows, away from the monster's gaze.

You know what it's saying?

I told you, that's one of the things under my bead.
I hear them all the time.
It's the same language.

You understand it?
After a while, yeah. They're always talking.

And that's what they look like?
They're usually a lot meaner looking.

This is impossible! How did it do that!?

It's like the ring projected the contents of the book!
It turns books into movies! That's awesome!

But how did Mr. Randolph get something like this?!
I told you he knows something about what's going on. This proves it!
But he can't help us now, you saw him!

Maybe there's something else in his office that'll explain everything.
We can't just walk in there. Miss Crowe is going to be watching us like a hawk.

Then for now, all we've got to go on is whatever is in this book.

Dudley, did the guy in the book say anything else?
He started to explain what they know about the monster and then he just stopped.

It looks like somebody has torn out the next several pages in the book.

That must be why he stopped talking, the pages aren't there. But where could they be?
And who has them now?

Come on, guys, we've got to find out everything we can about this book.

I've gone through the whole book at least twice...

And I still don't know what it has to do with anything.
Were you able to learn anything from it?

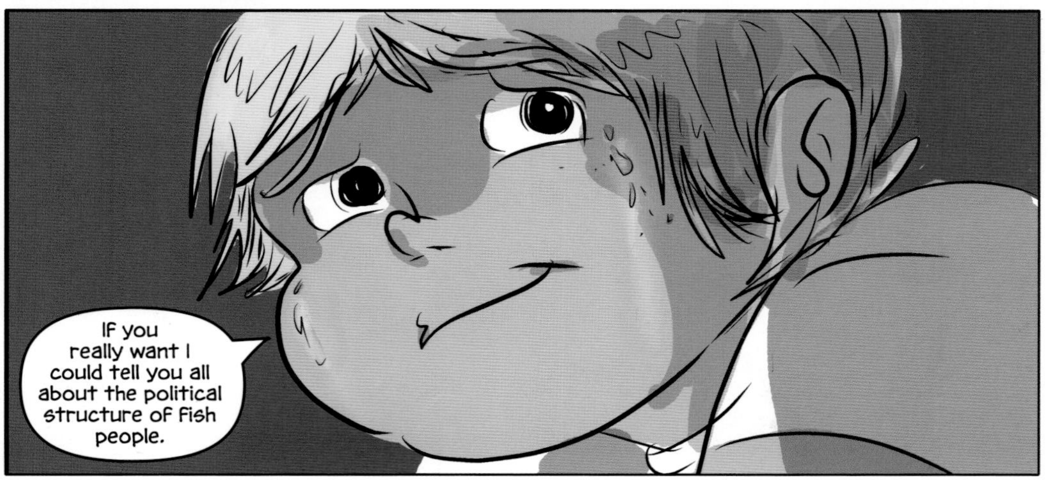
If you really want I could tell you all about the political structure of fish people.

Warren hasn't been able to find anything about Wa'Taar in the library.

I've also dug through my old issues of the Weekly Truth Journal...
I'd prefer to keep my references in the non-fiction category, thank you.

People who write for libraries aren't creative enough for this stuff.
Creativity has nothing to do with documenting facts!

Shows what he knows.

You three! Stop interrupting my class this instant!

As far as I can tell, Miss Crowe is watching the Welcoming Center like a hawk!

She or one of her Community Council cronies are always manning the desk.

We've still got to find a chance to check out Mr. Randolph's office.

I don't want to go anywhere near that place if Miss Crowe is there.

We still don't know what's on the missing pages.
It's probably more about that freaky monster thing.
TRASH

We can't know for sure without them.
It's hopeless, we'll never figure anything out at this rate!

We'll find something, we just need to look in the right place.

What are you kids doing here?

Lunch is over, you should be outside for recess!

Oh, Ms. Frump! We're... just working on a research paper!

That isn't one of our school books...
Where did you get this?

The library.

Don't lie to me, girl!

It's a book. Where else would we get it?

The cafeteria is closed to all students after lunch! You should all be at recess!

Unless you want an extra assignment to spend your time on instead!

Go! Go!

Too close for comfort.

Do you think she saw the book?
She asked us where we got it, of course she saw it!

But do you think she knows what it is?!

What if she tells Miss Crowe?!

What if the same thing that happened to Mr. Randolph happens to us?!

Calm down! Let's just get outside before she follows us.

Wait...

Does it seem really dark in here?

I'm going to lie and say no.
Let's just get out of here before Ms. Frump comes back.
Waugh!

It's after the book!
I've got it!

I can't touch it! It's like it's just a shadow!
It's got a heck of a grip for a shadow!

Let's see how it likes this.
Hey, it worked!
What was that thing?
Whatever it was...

...It looks like there's more of them coming!

They can't touch the book if it's in the light!

Ack!

Um...

I could really use that light right about now.

I can't aim it with this thing on me!

Dudley, quick! Throw me the book!

But I throw like a girl!

Shut up and do it!

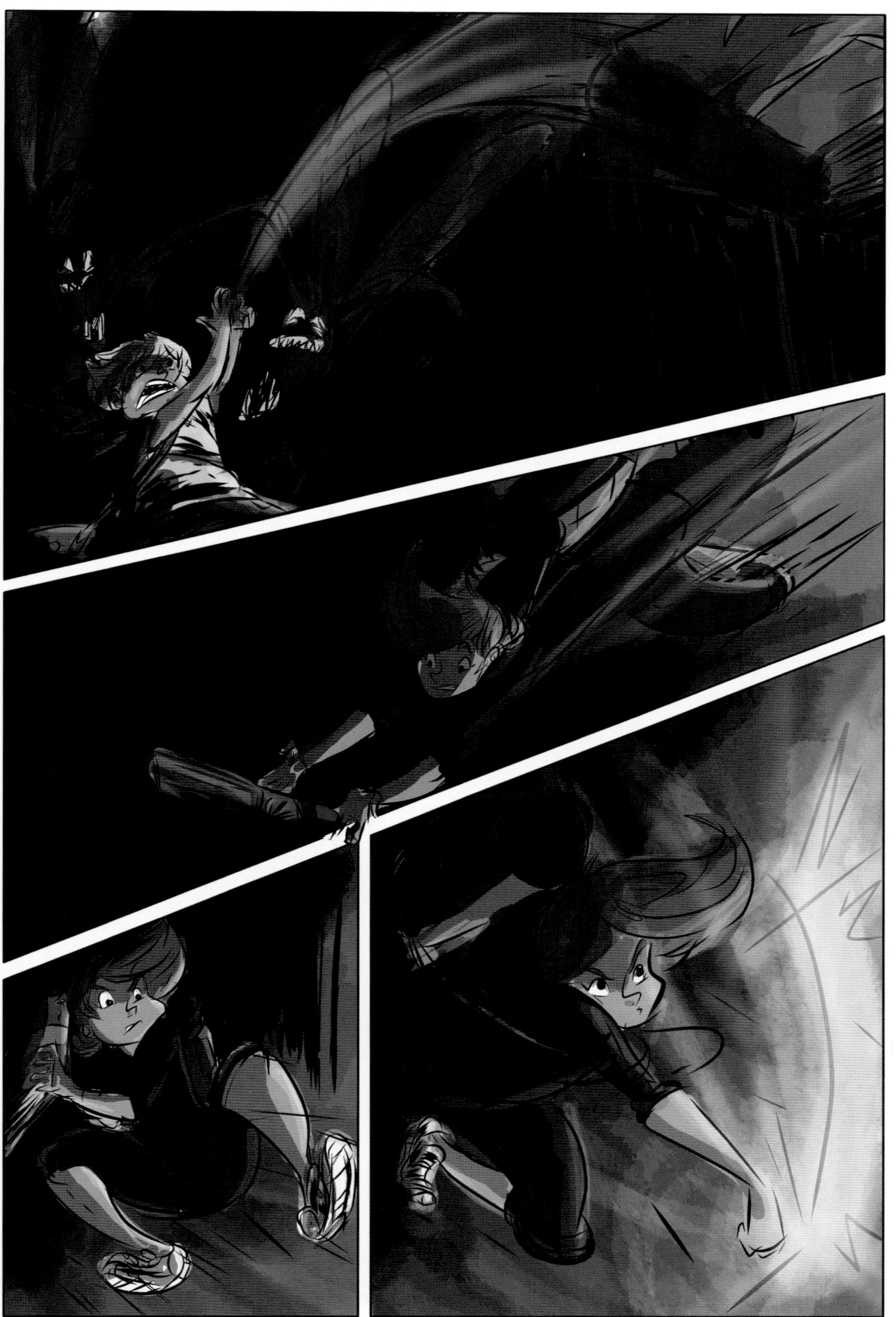

Now that's how a girl throws.

So, what are those things? Was there anything about them in the book?

I don't think so. All I read was mostly just slugs and Fishmen.

Whatever they are, they want that book. Which is reason enough for us to get it away from here.

Woah!
Warren!

TRASH

They're too fast! How many of those things are there?!

I don't know, I stopped looking after they attacked again!

Crazy cool monster or not, I could do without seeing those again.

I concur and propose we get out of here right now!

Grab the book and get outside!

I don't think they can come out here in the light.
Great, but what do creepy shadow bugs want with the book?

I don't think they do, they just don't want us to have it.
What?

They couldn't get the book, so they took the ring instead.
The logical explanation is that they don't want us to be able to read the book and they know we can't read it without the ring.

The book has to be important. First Ms. Frump throws a fit when she sees it, then those monsters!

Maybe Ms. Frump sent the monsters to steal the book!

You can't be serious.
I'm just saying.

Where is everybody? Isn't it recess?

Oh crap! We've missed recess entirely! Ms. Frump is going to kill us!
I don't want to go back in there.

Everything seems normal, all those weird shadows are gone.
We've got to get back, we're going to be in enough trouble as it is.

Well, well...

Look who finally decides to come back to class!

We're sorry Ms. Frump, we just–
I know exactly what you were doing!

You think your little extracurricular activities are more important than my class!
And for wasting my and the entire class' time waiting for you to come back...

...you've all just earned yourselves a stay in after-school detention tonight.
But Ms. Frump–

I don't want to hear any buts! And I don't want to see any more non-class-related materials in my classroom.

Am I understood?!
Hey! That's ours!

I'm sorry, is one night of detention not enough? Perhaps you would like a week?

Or maybe I should call your parents? Would you prefer that?
No, ma'am.

2 x 2 = 4
Then you'd all best take your seats, before I really get upset!

Thanks to you, I'm gonna miss all the good cartoons! There'll be nothing on but the news!

That show is so boring.

What is she doing in detention?
She's not allowed to walk home by herself.
I hate you forever plus forever!
There is to be no idle chitchat during detention!

Hrmph!

So, how do we get the book back from Ms. Frump?
Harley! We're in enough trouble as it is.

She sure seems interested in the book.
At least there's no way she can understand what's in there.

As far as we can tell it's written in some kind of Fishman language.

She couldn't possibly know how to read it.

Could she?

What're you reading?!

That's Carter's book! He won't let me read it, what's in it?!
I do not have patience for your frivolous questions, Miss Normandy.

Take your seat and remain silent!
I didn't do anything, it's not fair!

Polly, you can yell at me all you want when you get home. Just sit down, please.

You can't talk, you're in detention.

Polly, I really think you should listen to your brother.

He's
the one who
got in trouble,
not me!

Polly
Normandy!

Yes,
ma'am?
I have asked
you to be quiet,
and you continue to
misbehave! You have
earned yourself a
trip to special
detention!
Is that
better?

Come with me.

She's not even in your class.

The rest of you will sit and remain silent until we return or you'll all be facing detention for a week! Is that understood?

Can she do that?
Where is she taking her?
Wait, guys! Quiet!

Miss Crowe?!
What is she doing here?
Shhhh.

The ring! Ms. Frump has the ring!

It can't be! How could she get it?
What if Harley was right about her and those monsters?!
I couldn't be. I... I was just making stuff up!

She gave it to Miss Crowe.

But why?
They have both the ring and the book! This can't be good!
I'm gonna follow them. I can't let anything happen to Polly!
MATH

We're coming too!
We are?
No.

We know Miss Crowe is here at the school. That means she's not at the Welcoming Center!
Mr. Randolph knew she was up to something, and we need to find out what, fast!
You guys sneak into his office and find whatever you can, I'll keep an eye on Polly.
Right.

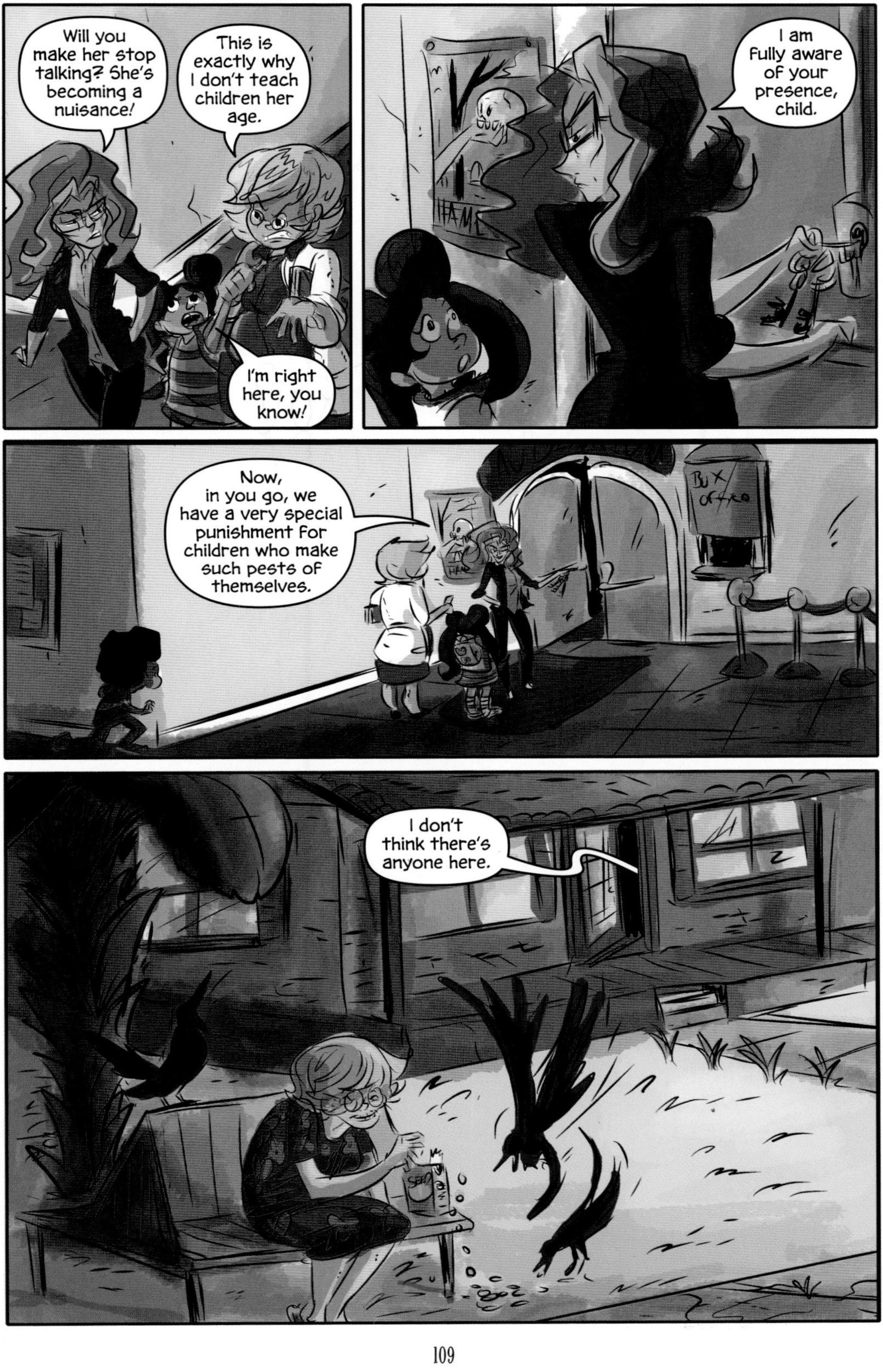

I don't think there's anyone here.

Good, now which one was Mr. Randolph's office?
I recall it being that one.
Warren, you go check it out, I'm going to see what dirt I can dig up on Miss Crowe.

What do I do?
Keep an eye on the door. Let us know if anyone's coming.

Oh, okay...

No problem.

Now sit here until I tell you otherwise.
I don't wanna!

If you do not do as you are told I will call your parents and you will be in even more trouble than you already are! Do you understand me, young lady?!

Hmph, you're just a big bully.

Ms. Frump, prepare to raise the curtain.

I will tend to the youth.

Found anything yet?

Mr. Randolph has a lot of books, but nothing out of the ordinary yet.

Oh. Harley?
Keep watching the door, Dudley!

And keep quiet, we don't want anyone to hear us!

Hello! What's this!

Holy crap!

I want to go home, I didn't do anything!

Why are you being so mean?

Are you listening to me?!

Child, you make it quite impossible not to listen to you with your constant supply of unnecessary noise.

But if you can not be made to be silent, you can at least be rendered to a state in which you are safely ignored.

Ms. Frump, raise the curtain now.

Dudley! Look at this!

What is it?!
It's the missing pages from the book!

In Miss Crowe's office?! What were they doing in there?!
Never mind that! Dudley, what does it say?

I don't know! I can't read it without the ring!

But I recognize that thing.

Woah!

There's no effect!
That's awesome!

Lower the curtain! It's not working!

Awwwwww.

I don't understand! It worked perfectly on Mr. Randolph!
This is a complete failure! The brat hasn't been affected at all. She's as obnoxious and rambunctious as ever.

That was so neat! It's like a giant spider flower lizard!

I don't know what could have gone wrong! Perhaps it doesn't work the same on children.
That is unacceptable! You have the book now, figure it out!
And great big wormy eyes!

What?!

That nosy girl and some of her friends have snuck into your office.

They're in there right now.

Keep an eye on them, don't let them leave. I'll be there immediately.

Keep an eye on the girl.

We've got someone sticking their nose where it doesn't belong.

Can I see the monster again?

Warren, have you found anything? We've got to get back to Carter and Polly!
I've found nothing useful, what's wrong?
We found the missing pages in Miss Crowe's office!

What?!
We can't read it, but it's definitely something about that monster from the book!

If that monster is really what messed up Mr. Randolph, then this proves Miss Crowe is behind it!

We're not going to get anywhere if we don't know what those pages say. If Mr. Randolph has another one of those rings hidden somewhere–

Forget that, we've got to get back to the school!

Eep!

That was Miss Crowe! I don't think she saw us.

She's bound to find us, we're trapped in here!
This is no time to panic!
She's right! This is a time to hide!

How very noble of you.
Quiet, she's inside!

Where are you intrusive, immature little cockroaches?
There's no reason we can't just talk like adults.

Who does she think she's kidding?
We don't have much choice, there's nowhere for us to go!

Not if we find a way out. Maybe there's a secret passage or something.
Don't be ridiculous! There's not going to be a secret—

I found a switch under Mr. Randolph's desk. did it do anything?
Dudley, you're awesome!
I am?

You'll probably never hear me say that again. Now come on!

Where are you hiding?

I hope Miss Crowe doesn't know about this room.
Woah! Look at all the stuff!

It looks like Mr. Randolph was doing some heavy duty research!

I want to see it again!

Sit down and be quiet! You're not seeing the creature again until I find out why it's not doing what it's supposed to.

Maybe if you didn't keep it all chained up it'd behave better!

It's not some pet to be coddled!
If I had a pet, like a big monster or a flying pony, I'd let it run wherever it wanted and never tie it up!

Quiet! You can't begin to understand what that creature is.
You just hate it. Just like you hate me, and hate everything else.

I have had enough of your lip, young lady.
Ow!
HEY!
Keep your hands off of my sister!

Carter!
What are you doing out of detention?!

Me?! What are you doing with a giant monster in the school auditorium?!

Don't you dare take that tone of voice with your teacher, young man.

Polly's right, you do hate everything. And you want to use that thing to get rid of everything you hate. You used it to do whatever you did to Mr. Randolph and now you want to use it on us!
I'm going to tell our mom that you're trying to scare us with a big monster!

Hah! Listen to yourselves. Do you really think anybody would believe such nonsense coming from children?
Mr. Randolph would believe us!
And where is Mr. Randolph?
That's right. Go back to your video games and your toys and leave the adult business to the adults.

You never know what things might be lurking in the dark.

Look at this stuff! Monsters... other dimensions... Mr. Randolph knows about all of this stuff.
Mmhmm.

Yeah.
Here's something about those shadow-fly things. It says they are subservient to he who summoned them, that must be Ms. Frump! What if she's a witch? I'm glad she's not our teacher next year.

And we've definitely not seen one of these things! What is it?
Are you even listening?

He's been there.
What? Been where?

The city from my dream, the one in the picture I took. This is it!

"Once we had grown accustomed to the more intricate means of dream travel, we then discovered this nameless abandoned city."
We? Who's we?
"It was there we discovered that miraculous ring which itself led to so many further discoveries."
"Two more were left behind, I have often thought of retrieving them if only to spare others from the burden of knowledge it has thus far revealed."
There's another ring!
Do you know what this is? This is correlating evidence!
I didn't just dream it, the city is real and this the first step towards actual legitimate proof!
Great, good to know you're not crazy. But we've got a more important question.
How do we get to that ring?
We have to find our way back to the dream city.
Guys, quiet! I think Miss Crowe is talking to someone out there!

You let them leave?!
We can't just hold them without their parents catching wind. Besides, they won't be talking. And if they do, nobody will believe them.

We can't take that risk! The ritual pages are missing!
What?
Those brats must have absconded with them. They're getting too close and are becoming a liability. They must be eliminated immediately.
But the creature has no effect.

On the children yes, so we aim at the source. With their parents reduced to babbling simpletons, we can have child services intervene and take their progeny far from Alabaster Shadows.

Frump! Call a conference with their parents at the school for tomorrow.

Those whelps can meddle all they want, they will be out of our hair soon enough.

This is bad.

Okay Polly, you go inside.
I wanna stay with you!

But I've got to go find the others. They might be–
You're staying right here, young man!

Mom! Dad!
We just got a very distressing call from your teacher.
I've never heard someone so upset!

I think she's always like that.
Polly!!

Well, it's true.

Your teacher has asked us to come to a parent-teacher conference tomorrow along with the parents of your new friends.
Is there anything you'd like to tell us before we hear it from her?

Carter saved me from a giant bug-eyed bug monster and Ms. Frump made a bunch of scary shadow goblin things but we ran away and came right back home!

Polly, this is no time for games! You are both grounded to your rooms until school tomorrow.
Yes sir.

And you can be sure we will be speaking with your teacher about this.
UBOX

Why didn't they believe me? I was telling the truth!

I know, but Ms. Frump is right, nobody will believe us.

It's not fair!
You're right, it's not. But it's the way things are.

I'm going to bed.

I've messed everything up!

Maybe there's still something you can do.

Dudley?

Is that you?
You're not going to give up that easy, are you?

Harley? All I've done is gotten us in trouble.

And I've dragged you all with me.

There's a reasonable solution for every problem.

But now our parents are in danger!
They didn't even do anything!

Then fix it, Carter! You're supposed to watch out for me!

Polly?!

What the heck is going–

–on?

Ah, Mister Normandy! You've Finally made it!

What is this place?

Where is this?

Is this a dream?
Yes, I suppose it is. But not one of your own. Everything before the door was yours, of course. It looks like you're feeling guilty.

Because of me, everyone is–
Don't!

You should never feel guilty over the pursuit of knowledge. It's the most noble goal a man can strive for!

Then how did I end up here?
The only way to end up anywhere in the Dreamscape is to want whatever is at your destination. So the real question is...

...what do you want?

I don't know.

Let's look at your friends, see where they ended up.
They're here too?

Not here exactly, but in the broad sense, they are indeed.

First is the brash one.

She wanted to see that there is something out there beyond even her vivid imagination.

And believe me, there is always something else beyond imagination to be found.

And the quiet one. It appears more than anything else, he wanted to be somewhere safe.

Is that just his room?
Oh no, there are no monsters under that bed.

There are really monsters under his bed?
There are monsters everywhere.

Finally is your friend the skeptic.

He wanted to go back to his forgotten city.

To get the same result from a repeated experiment.

Like the others, he found himself precisely where he wanted.

Now this brings us back to you. What is it that you wanted?

I don't know! I don't know why I ended up here.
Of course you do.

What's the one thing you want more than anything else?
I don't even know what this place is!

What have you been looking for this whole time? What is it? Tell me!

I want answers!

There you go.

And that's why I found you?

Absolutely. Now then, what answers are you looking for?

I need to know how to save my parents!
Really?
I show you all of this and all you care about is preserving what you already know?

They're my family!
Your friends already have all the pieces you need, you just need to put them together.

What do you mean? How do I do that?
Just because I have answers doesn't mean I'm in any way obliged to give them to you.

Besides, the discovery is half the fun.

Fun?! Something bad is happening and I don't know what is going to happen if I don't find a way to stop it!

But don't you want to find out?
NO!

That's your prerogative. Me, I think it's fascinating!
Who are you?

Nobody.

Ms. Frump is having the parent-teacher conference today after school. We've got to come up with a plan before then.
What kind of plan?

I don't know yet. Warren, you found another one of those rings in your dream last night, does it work?

How did you know—
I saw you all in my dream. I know it sounds crazy, but we don't have time to worry about that!
Yes, it works just like the old one.

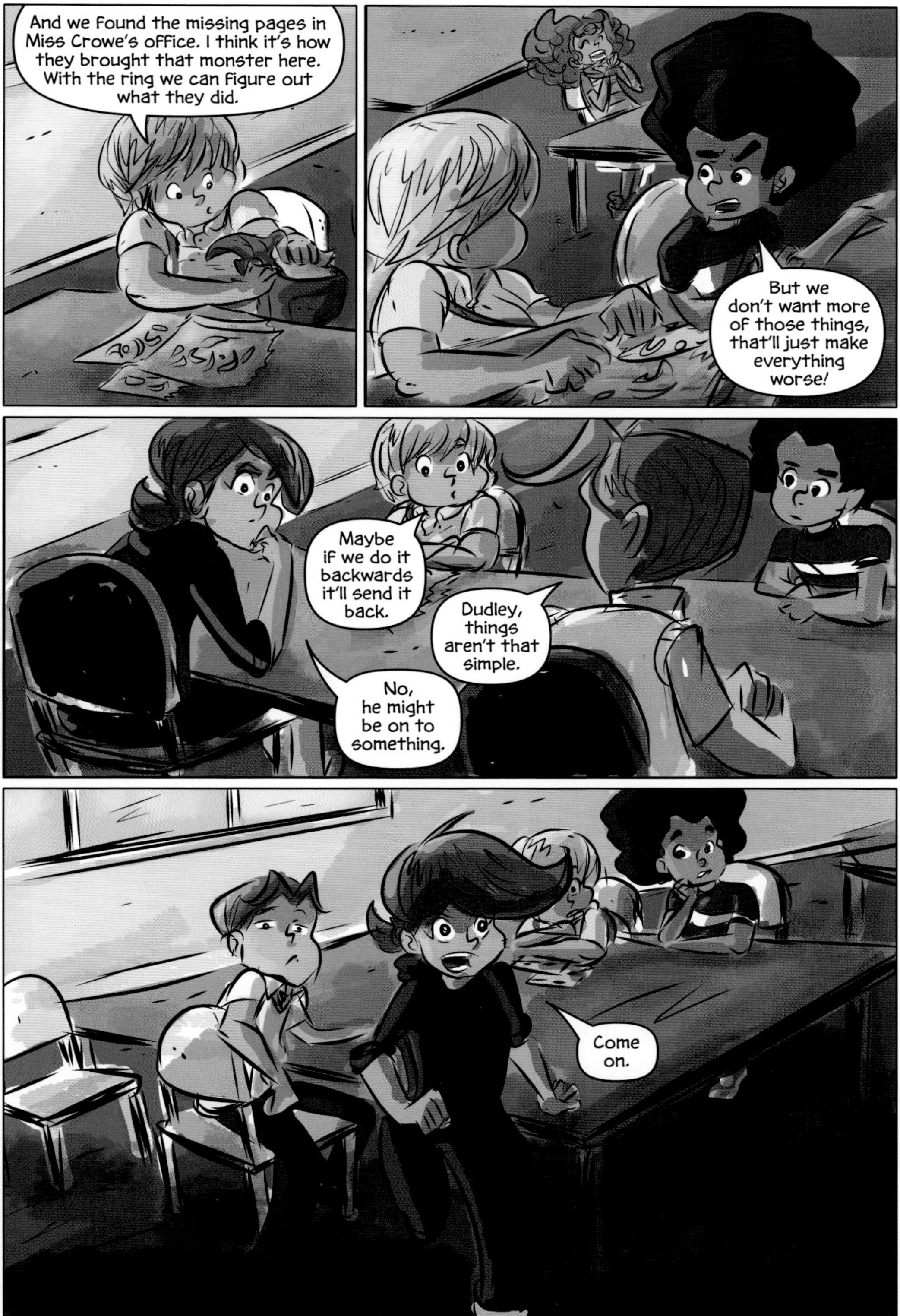

And we found the missing pages in Miss Crowe's office. I think it's how they brought that monster here. With the ring we can figure out what they did.

But we don't want more of those things, that'll just make everything worse!

Maybe if we do it backwards it'll send it back.
Dudley, things aren't that simple.
No, he might be on to something.

Come on.

One of these issues of the Weekly Truth Journal has an article about reversing curses. I keep it just in case I meet a witch that doesn't like me.
Do you have every issue in there?
Just two years' worth.

Here it is!

Granted, this is more of a summoning than a curse but it should work in a pinch!

Lunch is over, we've got to get to class so Ms. Frump doesn't get suspicious. Meet me behind the auditorium right after class.

We've got to get rid of that thing before our parents can see it!

Thank you
for coming on
such short notice.
It's unfortunate that these
conferences must always
be under such dreadful
circumstances.

Isn't this
place a bit
large for such
a small
meeting?
Our regular
conference rooms
are under renovations,
but the auditorium
seats are much more
comfortable.

She's
already taking
everybody
inside. We've got
to hurry!

Quiet Back ENTRANCE
How is that lock coming along, Harley?
Got it!

Quick, get inside before anyone sees us!

Is... is that it?

Woah!

Yeah, they've got it trapped here somehow. I don't think it wants to be here any more than we want it to be.

Do we have any reason to believe this is going to work?
Not really, but it's the only plan we've got. Dudley, get the pages ready.

Greetings, everyone!

If you're wondering why I'm here let me assure you that we at the Community Council take an active role in all aspects of our residents' lives.

Especially where our dear children are involved.

What's it saying?
I can't hear with you talking like that!
Okay, I think I've got it, first it says to make a large circle of salt around the area.
There's already one around the monster there!

Uh, he says the last step is to open the "vessel of cosmic energies."

What is that supposed to be?

Is it that thing?
It's just a jar... that's disappointing.
They must've been working with whatever they had.

What do I do with it?

I dunno, close it I guess.
You don't know?!

Okay.

Nothing happened.
This isn't going to work.
Shut up, Warren. Dudley, what's next?
Uh, let me check...

And as you know the proper education of our community's children is of the utmost importance.

To this effect, Ms. Frump has prepared a presentation to illustrate her plan for the regrettable subject of discipline.

If you would please raise the curtain.
Certainly.

No, the red one goes here! Put the blue one over there!

Can I just reiterate how uncomfortable I am being this close to that thing?
Hurry up, we're almost done. What's next!

Next is...

What's that noise?

The curtain's rising!

Oh no! We're too late!
Keep going, you'll need this!
Buying some time!
Where are you going?

If everyone will look closely onstage—

CLICK

What is going on? Argh!

Ack!

I apologize, there seems to be some sort of electrical failure, as soon as things are back up we'll be right back on schedule.

Got it.

What the heck?!

You meddling brats!
I'm sure Ms. Frump will have everything restored momentarily so we may—
Undomesticated little mongrels!
If you'll excuse me momentarily.

You think you can actually stop this?

There is nothing you can do!

This is bigger than you can comprehend!

We know exactly what you're doing. You're using the monster to turn everyone you don't like into zombies!

This is about far more than just you, your parents, or even this insignificant little town!

What is going on over there? I can't see anything.

I should've expected you to be behind this, Normandy!

I won't let you hurt my parents!

What can you possibly do, child?

Besides, I don't think it'll actually hurt.

No!

There is nothing anyone can do, it is only a matter of–
...

She looked right at it.

Did she?

The curtain's moving again!

On it!

It worked! I can't believe it actually worked!
We've gotta get out of here before they see us!

I can
understand technical
difficulties and all, but
this is a bit excessive
for a parent-teacher
conference.

at the
center of all
existence, from the
swirling unending
nothing

What's going on, what just happened?

It's gone! How did you–?

We may be kids, but you shouldn't have underestimated us. We're going to find out exactly what you're up to!

countless things from beyond the cosmos, devouring all before them

You may think you've won, you conniving little whelp! But nobody is going to believe a thing you say! You're nothing but a child! A worthless, insignificant, petulant child!

the piping music of cleansing madness echoes into eternity

I am so terribly sorry about what appears to be nothing more than a cruel prank. I assure you the Community Council had no idea about this.

And the one responsible will be severely reprimanded.

Please disregard any nonsense Ms. Frump may have said regarding your children or otherwise.

She is clearly very unwell.

I can't believe something from that ridiculous magazine of yours actually worked!
We did it!
To be honest I was just winging half of it!
What's important is that Miss Crowe can't use that thing to hurt our parents anymore.
Carter!
Polly?! What are you doing here?

There's something big going on, and I think Mr. Randolph was trying to stop it.
We're getting in way over our heads.
Maybe, but we've just proven that we don't have to just sit back and do nothing.
And the Council may have the book, but we've got the monster pages!
It's as good a place as any to start.
We've got Mr. Randolph's notes.
We just need to keep digging, find out what is going on and what we can do about it.
And find more neat monsters!

I could do without more monsters, thank you.
The monsters are the coolest part!
I think I'm with Warren on this one.

For now, we should get home. Our parents are heading back now.
We'll meet up at school tomorrow.

Let's go home.

From the
inky blackness,
undulating
amorphous
creatures...

...effortlessly
maneuvering through
matter as though
immaterial...

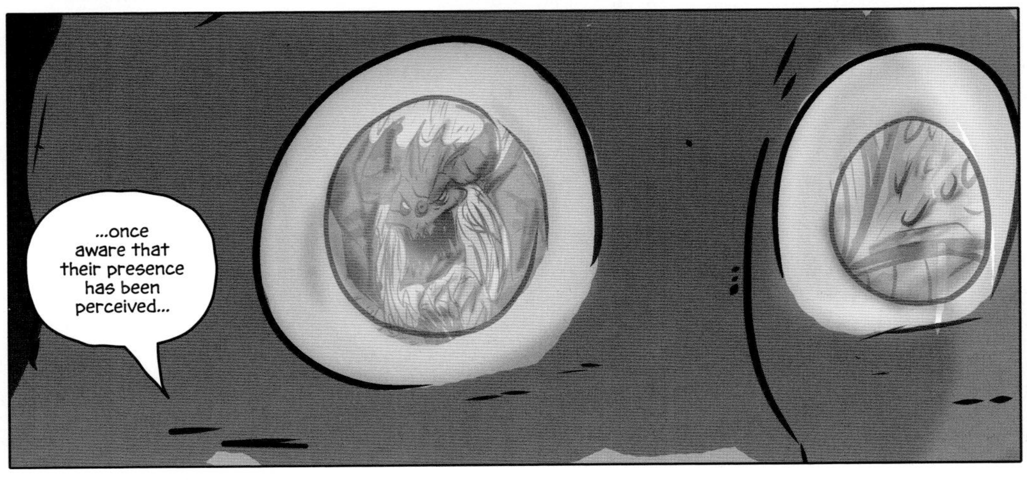
...once
aware that
their presence
has been
perceived...

...the beings become then aware of the perceiver...

SKETCH GALLERY

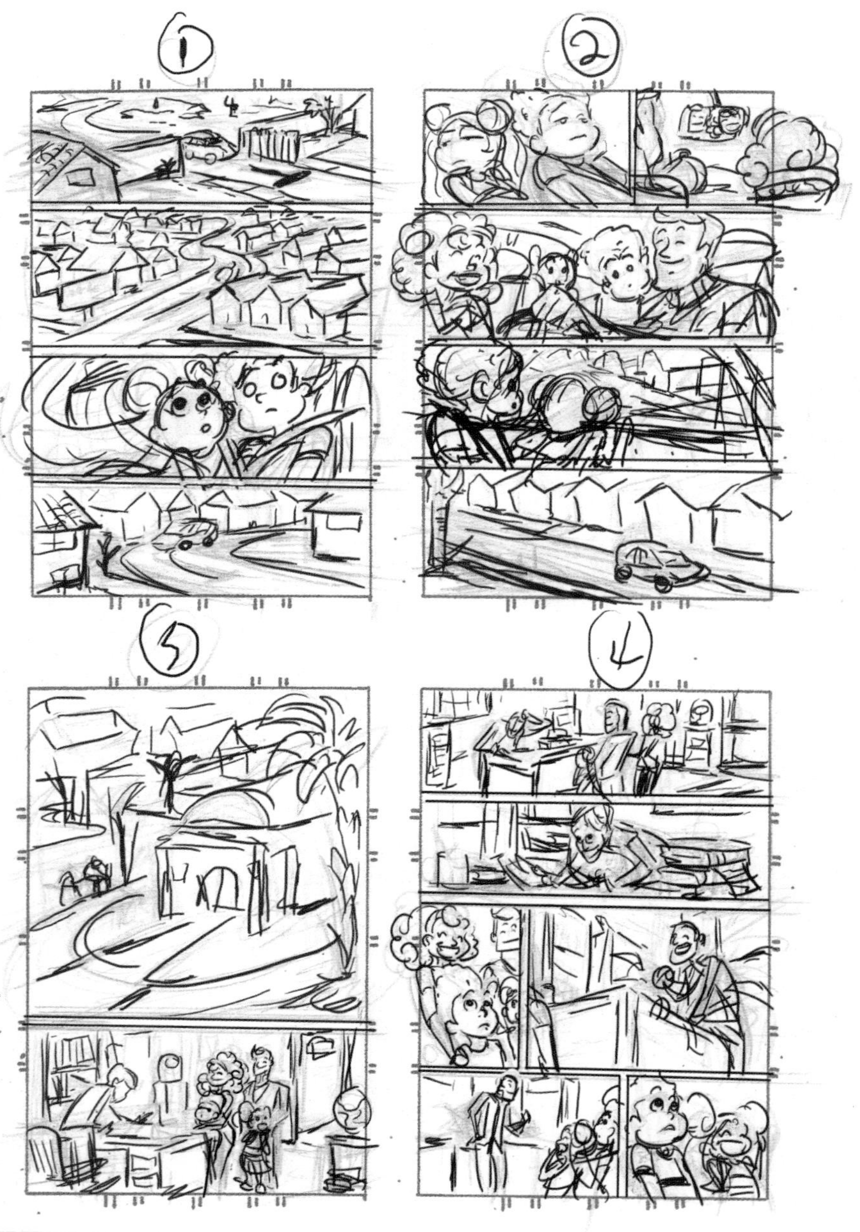
1
2
3
4

I HATE CHILDREN!

SHADOWFLIES
EMERGE FROM SHADOWS.
ABOUT THE SIZE OF BIG CATS
OR SMALL DOGS. POSSIBLY ALWAYS
TETHERED TO SOME SHADOW.

MATT GARDNER

is a writer, voice actor, animator and creator of Floating Hands Studios. An avid devourer of comics, cartoons and TV since childhood, he's eager to tell the sort of stories that inspired him at an early age. He's humbled that Oni Press saw enough potential in his cartoons to give him the opportunity to write this book. Also he would like to thank his peers, mentors and family for always encouraging him to work at what he loves and keep writing.